I0620762

1

You Don't Know Me

Me

by rainbo b. seed

Book One

When The Stars

Whisper Your Name

You Don't Know Me
Book One: When The Stars Whisper Your Name
Copyright © 2019 by r g cantalupo (aka rainbo b. seed)

All rights reserved. No part of this book may be reproduced or transmitted in any form or by any means without written permission from the author.

ISBN (9781733288309)

Published in USA by New World Publishers
www.newworldpublishers.com

You don't know me...

...but I ain't who you think I am.

I ain't red or yellow or black or brown or white.
I'm all those colors and more!
I'm green if I want to be.
Green like one of those lime-green frogs they have in Africa that shoots

poison from its
tongue.

Or green like one
of those preying
mantises that are
stone-still till some
unsuspecting beetle
comes walking up
the vine—then Zap!
ain't nothing left
except a hole in the
sky where one less
beetle used to be!

Or green like one
of those wild, lime-

green parrots I see flying through the turquoise sky from time to time.

But if I were green, someone might call me an alien, and who knows what would happen to me.

Grandma says I'm all those colors and more because I'm the granddaughter

of the First Peoples
of the World.

'Course I don't
take everything
grandma says as
fact, being as she
communes with
spirits and ghosts
and the like.

Besides, what
grandma says ain't
always in the words,
but in the notion of
what she's meaning—

(if you know what I mean!)

One thing for sure: I know nothing about The World.

The World's about as strange to me as you sitting there reading this story however long it's been since I first done the writing.

The World's about as unfathomable as trying to see the

moon and stars in a pebble I found rolling around the bottom of my shoe, or trying to figure out where that pebble originally came from, or why it gave me such a blister for walking on its gnarly head.

I mean--snakes alive!--how am I supposed to know The World, when I can't even tell you why the sky is blue, or where my freckles come from, or what makes the moon change into jack o' lantern faces each night.

Most of the time, I don't even know who I am, let alone all those people I see on you tube, or tv, or read about in the magazines mama brings home from those offices she cleans in the nighttime.

Most days, I'm lucky if I know my own name let alone all the names that's been given to the children of the First Peoples of the World.

Which reminds me, I ain't told you who I am yet have I?

I do that.

I get so caught up in the telling some-times I forget to tell what people wants to know first.

So...

I'm Rainbo.

Rainbo B. Seed.

Rainbo after all them colors I done told you 'bout and B after Bwana, a great African Princess.

Bwana means beautiful in Swahili, least that's what my mama says, and you don't be crossing mama when she tells you such a thing.

Mama be coming at you like one of them Medusa heads with all the serpent mouths snapping at you from multitudinous directions if you done try and argue with something she knows as fact.

Anyways, I ain't so beautiful with my pink freckles and my red hair that's so curly even my curls got curlicues.

So no, I don't go by Bwana.

I just go by Rainbo, or Rainbo B., or Rainbo B.

Seed if people want to be formal.

The Seed's after my father, but I ain't seen him since I was in the middle of my first crib escape.

Come to think of it, that's the very last time I did see him, when I had a leg over the top of my crib, trying to climb over the side, and he came and grabbed me and picked me up high over his head and flew me around like one of the wooden birds circling 'round my crib.

No, I ain't seen him since he left me there, sitting in my crib, giving me one of those sad smiles he always gave when he didn't know what else to do.

Then he turned 'round and shut the bedroom door behind him, and I ain't never seen him since.

'Course I can't tell you that story yet.

I can't tell you that story 'cause it wouldn't make no sense without the in-betweens.

(See, as far as I know, there ain't no story without no in-betweens, and there ain't no in-betweens without no story to put them in-between.)

Okay.
So I think we're done with all that, "How are ya? Happy to meet ya." stuff.

What's important is, I ain't no witch, and neither is my grandma.

I mean Pooff!, I couldn't turn you into a toad even if I wanted to.

That's black magic bizness and, like I said, I'm no witch, not even a white one!

I'm a whisperer.

A snake-whisperer.

I know, you ain't never heard of no snake-whisperer.

You've heard about horse-whisperers and dog-whisperers and elephant-whisperers and monkey-whisperers and dolphin-whisperers.

Maybe you even heard of whisperers who whisper to the whisperers in such

soft sweet sounds
that even butterflies
and bees can hear
their whispers as
they flitter from
flower to flower.

There's even goat-
whisperers though I
don't know who'd
want to whisper to
those knobby-
headed monsters or
what language them
whisperers be
whispering in

beyond "baaah, baaah, baaah" and the like.

But snakes—that's a leap of faith across the Grand Canyon of your imagination!

I was born with the gift of hearing the suspirating voices of the reptilian realm, and ithat's the upside down of it!!!

Somehow the reptilian part of my brain got tuned in to the reptilian part of reptiles' brains and I could hear everything they thought and said under their whispering breaths. It was like I was on the wave-length of some radio station only I could hear.

And if it happened I won "America's Got Talent" and became famous and helped the Snake Clan to fly, well, that happened more by accident than by sorcery.

Uh oh!!!

Someone's knocking on my door.

...?
...?
...?

Okay.
I think we're safe...

See, I ain't supposed to be writing this.
'Cause I'm kinda under house arrest.
With the F-B-I.

You can see them
parked outside my
front   window,
sitting   in   that
unmarked car.

Yeah.
That's   them
alright.
With   the   square
jaws and short hair
like Bart Simpson.
Watching.
Watching,   and
listening.

They call it Witness Protection!

'Cept I ain't no witness and I sure don't feel protected. Not from Ivan Putinovitz and his Russian goons.

But I ain't about to keep quiet so long as those news people keep spreading lies about me and my family--

secret identity or no secret identity!

And since I'm the only one doing the telling, and you're the only one doing the listening, this story's 'bout as 'true to life' as it gets.

It's like you and me's holding hands, walking down the path of my life story!

So, take my hand!

Let's go!!!

Snakes...

...that's how it all began.

With a snake.

Now I know girls ain't supposed to like snakes being as snakes are all slippery and slimy an' all. But I been likin' snakes ever since I first climbed over my crib bars and started crawlin'.

Truth is, snake was the first creature I met when I explored the circumference of my world.

Before spiders, worms, rats, flies, mosquitoes, centipedes, and every other kind of creepy crawly insect, reptile, or furry animal, what I seen was snake.

And the thing was I wasn't scared then and I ain't scared now—and girlness gots nothin' to do with it!

So as I was sayin'--or maybe I was sayin' this 'fore you came in and so you didn't hear me—"I was crawlin' down the bedroom highway, goin' toward my mama's voice (which was comin' from the kitchen), when I took a wrong turn and ended up inside a closet lookin' up at mama's clothes."

Coats with boas, dresses with white and yellow and black stripes like tigers and zebras, chartreuse blouses with cockatoos—mama's closet was a menagerie of nightly creatures she slipped inside to saunter across the dance floor on Saturday nights and boogie her body in a blissful mambo.

Lookin' upside at them animals made me dizzy as an upside down stink bug, besides somethin' owned my hand and was keepin' it from movin' forward. When I looked down I found my fingers half-gone inside a mouth.

Now if'n I didn't have keen eyes, I mighta believed that shoe had eaten my fingers an' maybe started screamin' for mama to save me. But I knew 'bout teeth and chewin' from mama's calico cat.

"Calipso" mama called her, and she had a fierce nibblin' thing for my fingers so I knew what chewin' felt like and this shoe-creature weren't chewin' 'cause he didn't have no teeth.

See, after dresses, mama loved shoes—red and black, silver and brown, stilettos and flats, patent leather working shoes and shoes for jiggin' to the mambo, shoes with pointy noses and shoes with mouths wide as sharks, shoes long and slender and elegant as dreamboats, and shoes glitterin' with green and blue rhinestones pretty as Cinderella slippers I seen in fairytales.

Them rhinestone ones was the ones that held me though.

I never seen such a happy twinklin' unless it be that jeweled butterfly mobile my grandma give me.

Her butterfly hung above my bed and sparkled as she flew through the blue sky of my ceilin', and try as I might to catch it as it twirled round and round I never was able to touch those silvery sparklin' wings.

So that's why mama's silver rhinestone pumps was so allurin' an' why I reached out to try and grab one.

'Course I could see right off somethin' weren't right 'cause there was two shadows and one was movin' forward and one was movin' back and one was my hand and one was who knows what. But it sure weren't mine, and somethin' movin' that weren't mine was scary enough, let alone it bein' somethin' I never seen nor heard 'bout before.

I mean they don't have snakes in them fairytale books.

Oh, they got's lots of frogs and sheep and mices, but I ain't never heard of no snake in one of them stories. Maybe they didn't have no snakes in that part of the country where those tales be takin' place or maybe the teller just leave out the snake part 'cause of their bad reputation and all and 'cause they always seem to take over a story no matter what the body doin' the tellin' wants to emphasize.

But the thing was, since I ain't never seen no snake, I ain't 'bout to know what a snake look like. So when I done seen that shadow movin', why I just naturally grabbed for it bein' as maybe it was one of them shoe-creatures runnin' away from my hand.

No, I seen that black shadow sculkin' in the corner as a good omen. I mean there was just me and him crawlin' around and them shiny shoes with the funny faces. 'Sides, when I reached out and snatched him, he was the wigglingest shadow I ever had in my hands and seemed more afraid of me than I was of him, 'specially with his head wrapped inside my tiny fist and my big chocolate eyes looking into his beady blacks.

Most people thinks snakes don't have no expression, but I seen right off that if'n he weren't so spooked by his neck bein caught in my hand, he woulda been a'grinnin'.

'Cause that's what snakes do.

They been grinnin' and a'grinnin since the first day the cosmos be born. Grinnin' is their natural expression; grinnin', and gloomin'.

You can't look at their crescent-shaped mouths facin' you dead on without seein' the grin there 'less them lip lines be turned down and they got a bad case of the blues like down-on-their-luck people's got on their sad faces. 'Course maybe that's why most people don't see their expressions, 'cause people be lookin' at snakes sideways and can't see the angle of their emotions. Either way, ain't nothing to be scared of less you be scared of your own face lookin' back at you.

So I be holdin' his head in my hand and lookin' at him all clear-eyed with wonderment, and what's he do?

He goes and sticks his slithery tongue out at me and runs it along his thin lips like he just ate the sweetest bug you ever seen.

Well, I just stick my tongue back out at him an' we just went on and on like that, stickin' out tongues and grinnin', till he curled his cool body round my arm and I started talkin' my own special language, and he looked at me sideways, and then starts to whisper all soft and smooth.

Now I s'ppose me and him coulda gone on conversin' like that till the blue moon rise over the Black Mountains, but mama done hear our whisperin' and started wonderin' who I be talkin' with if it weren't with myself—(oh, I forgot to tell you, mama's got ears like an elephant. Grandma says mama's ears so sensitive they can hear the grass grow even when there ain't no sun to give it inspiration.)

Anyway, she sneaks in quiet as a stalkin' cat and when she sees Mr. Snake curled round my arm, she lets out such a God-fearin' scream both Mr. Snake and I nearly had a heart seizure.

He got so terrified, he whirled off my arm, squirted out of my palm, and dove into a little crack in the floor.

But mama was already on him, whackin' away at where he was slitherin' with one of her boots, and if it weren't for him being so quick, and mama being such a bad swinger, he woulda been squished sure as I'm sittin' here.

After that mama comes and scoops me up like she was one of them giant pterodactyls and puts me back inside my crib.

Well, I have to tell you, I got's the anger going so deep inside me by now, I just starts a'wailin and a'rattlin those bars so loud and strong, she don't know what to do with me, so she runs and gets a bottle of warm, honey-milk and tries to stick it between my lips.

But this just gets me ragin' even more, so I take's that bottle and throws it at her.

That done it all right!

Now she's so exasperated she just sits down on the floor and starts cryin'.

She cries and cries, but when she finally looks up, she sees me smilin' at her, so she gets all quiet and serious and stops cryin' and comes and picks me up and holds me in her arms. She starts kissin' my face with them wet puckery kisses and starts singin' to me in that coo coo coo chirpy bird kinda language, and, after awhile, I can't help but laugh and forgive her for scarin' me and Mr. Snake half-to-death.

By then she realizes I'm all wet in my bottom part from all the excitement, so she lays me down on the floor and washes me up with that warm perfumy water with them pretty bubbles an' foamy sudsy sponges. Then she sprinkles that soft sweet powder all over my body and I'm so flower-smellin' happy

I let her put that milk bottle back inside my mouth.

My eyes start gettin' heavy and begin to close, and soon I'm seein' Mr. Snake again, and he's curled up on my shoulder, and he's lickin' my face like a happy kitten and grinnin' from ear to ear, and when I wake up I'm back in my crib with the blankets laid over me and my bottle beside me same as when mama left me.

I knowed then that Mr. Snake and I's gonna be friends for a good, long time, and mama's probably always gonna be afraid of him, and I gots to keep our friendship secret 'cause who

knows what bad thing she
might do to him in her fear.

So, that's how...

...me and Mr. Snake got to be friends.

Weren't too long after that he started introducin' me to his whole family and all his relatives and by the time mama figured out a new way to constrain me I already knew all Mr. Snake's children and where his home was and what he ate for breakfast most mornings.

'Course I had to keep this all a secret mind you 'cause mama woulda slapped Mr. Snake upside the head with a broom if'n she woulda spotted him again. So for awhile I just visited him every so often when he come slippin' in to the closet or come up through that old crack in the floor in the corner of my bedroom.

After a time, when we got to be good friends, he'd come visit me in my crib slitherin' up through the bars. He'd come and we'd stick out tongues and be grinnin' and then he'd crawl up my arm and curl round tight and sway his head back and forth like he was dancin'. Then I would start whisperin' and he would nod and sway his head this way and that as if he understood exactly what I was sayin'.

Now I knowed mama wouldn't understand all this talkin' and sharin' secrets and tellin' Mr. Snake my dreams and such, so I kept my sharin' to myself.

But if'n it weren't for the snake-whisperin' I wouldn't be

havin' to tell you this here story in the first place.

See the snake whisperin' is what got me into trouble right from the beginnin' 'cause they ain't so many people be wantin' to talk to snakes in the first place an' seems there weren't nobody fool enough to think they could communicate with the reptilian world let alone teach a snake to fly. But that's why they put me on "America's Got Talent" in the first place and that's why you probably seen my face in the newspapers and on tv.

But I'm getting ahead of where I'm supposed to be.

All that celebrity stuff happened later and happened by

accident. I mean it weren't like I invented snake-flying or nothin', (though I guess some people think's I did. That's where the truth gets crooked and that's what I'm tryin' to straighten out here.)

See the thing was, in the beginnin', Mr. Snake and I was just gettin' to be friends and weren't thinkin' 'bout no future or that we were the first snake and human to be communicatin' on a whisperin' level. I mean me and him just be grinnin' and tongue waggin' and there weren't a whole lot to our story tellin' 'cept me babblin' 'bout life in the crib (which didn't amount to much), and him tellin' me 'bout the dangers of bein' a snake, and how each day there was some new creature tryin' to gobble up him or one of his family like they was worms or somethin'.

I say my life didn't amount to much, but at the time findin' shiny coins and colored buttons and paper clips and tin foil and hairpins and what have yous was a wonder. Mama didn't like my crawlin' expeditions too much and soon got one of them fancy playpens for when I escaped from my crib. She just swooped down on me and plopped me in the playpen which was really just a bigger crib with taller fences.

'Course the playpen only worked long enough for me to figure out how to pull my leg over the side and hang onto the bar and pull the rest of my body over.

Mama thought all them rattles and furry animals and noisy balls and colored blocks would keep me occupied, but there weren't nothin' too excitin' 'bout a bunch of loud inanimate objects after visitin' with Mr. Snake and his family.

See the thing is, I ain't much for loud noises.

Give me soft whispers and bits of conversations comin' through the walls or under doorways or siftin' through windows and I be happy as a night-crawler in heaven.

Give me sounds and snippets of words floatin' down like

pieces of confetti 'fore loud bleeps and blares and shouts all day all night three hundred and sixty-six days a year.

Give me...

Well, you gets the idea.

So I guess in that regard I always been a whisperer of sorts and maybe that man on the television was right when he called me a natural-born snake-whisperer.

Anyways, you knowed that playpen wasn't gonna hold me for long with my talent for climbing, so after I been escapin' from my playpen on a regular basis for awhile mama done hooked a harness round me an' tied me to a leg of the kitchen table.

I guess I could've been offended by her new kinda incarceration bein' I wasn't a dog or a monkey or other such domestricated bein'. But it turned out that leash was no more restrictin' than them tall fences she tried keepin' me inside.

See by now I could do all sorts of fancy crawlin' and climbin' to continue my adventures.

I could caterpillar my way up stairs and over boxes and up and over tables and across rivers of record albums and cleaning supplies and such.

I could prop myself up on two arms and waddle my behind like a duck and trundle through the hall.

I could push my body up and down and do the sun-bathin lizard and gaze out over the horizon of shoes and boxes and what-have-yous.

I could wiggle and flop and lug my belly across the floor like a blubbery sea elephant, and I could wobble and joggle and doddle my head around and do the bobble-head-doll crawl, and I could grab and clutch and hang onto whatever was there to hold myself up.

I ain't gonna say that weren't a problem sometimes, 'cause not everythin' wants to be grabbed onto and climbed over and happen to be there just to hold me up while I be doin' my special crawls. I mean I done tipped over a few lamps and toppled more'n my share of chairs and bookcases and record stands. But most of the time them objects be faring a whole lot better than me, and I be the one that'd be fallin' on my behind rather than them be a'fallin'.

Now you probably already know this, but there ain't nothin' harder than one day getting' up on your own two feet like the rest of the human species rather than crawlin' around on your all fours. I don't know who ever come up with the idea of humans havin' to lope around like gorillas or sasquatch rather than do the monkey-walk, but whoever it was must of forgotten what it was like to be one-years old. I had a hard enough time keepin' my head wobblin' in the right direction let alone keepin' my legs and arms movin' together like they belonged to the same person 'steada some inebriated soul.

So like I said I didn't mind the harness much. Kinda helped me climb 'cause I had somethin' to grab onto when there weren't nothin' else to hold. Didn't stop me from visitin' with Mr. Snake and the rest of his family when I wanted though. I could wobble and crawl on over to my secret corner and mama wouldn't be none the wiser. She'd be thinkin' I was playin' with one of them inanimate objects she put in my playpen (like I was gonna have a conversation with a raggedy anne who never said nothin' but looked at me with those glassy eyes and ever-present happy-face smilin' from her patchwork skin.)

My secret corner was where me and Slim, (Slim was Mr. Snake's first name, the one his friends called him), met up and did our tongue waggin' and grinnin' and whisperin'. Was a little hole in the corner of my bedroom where I could stick my little finger through the hole and wiggle it 'round under the floor which meant I was free and Slim could come visit. Musta looked like another snake to Slim with my finger wigglin' at him through a hole in the floor.

I don't know how long our secret meetings went on. Seems

like they went on through Summer and into the Fall, long enough for me to meet all of Slim's family and relatives down to the last baby snakes that was no more'n a week old and hadn't even been named yet, and I don't know how long Mama be gettin' suspicious 'bout me goin' off and playin' by myself without makin' nary a peep for who knows how long, but one day mama done slipped in all nice and quiet while we be a'whisperin' and a'grinnin and let out a howl like you ain't heard since the first baby done howled her original cry upon wakin' up in this strange new world. She let out such a high-pitched sound a bathroom mirror cracked and the birds over my crib started flyin' round and round like they was being chased by a hungry crow.

I never saw Slim tear himself away from my arm so fast. He dived down into the crack in the floor 'fore mama could even grab for that broom of hers and start whackin', and everythin' woulda been fine if it weren't for Slim's nephew who was visitin' with us that day and who happened to be a bit farsighted (which ain't so great when you be needin' to find a small crack in the floor to escape through.) Mama was a'whackin' and a'screamin' and Shadows, (that was Slim's nephew's name, Shadows. I guess they named him that 'cause he spent most of his time in the dark and 'cause he couldn't see nothin' in the sun but shadows.) Anyway, Shadows was slitherin' and twistin' and jumpin' every which way but sideways tryin to get out of the path of mama's swing and he were 'bout as close to findin' that crack that led back to where his home was as mama was to getting' rich and famous on "American Idol".

And then the darnest thing happened. Mama swung and somehow catched Shadows on the tail with the broom, and Shadows just glommed on to the end of that broom like he was ridin' a bushy-tailed buckin' bronco or somethin'.

'Course mama was way past beside herself by now. She couldn't figure out no how where

Shadows be gone to. I mean there was no way she be fathomin' he done slipped onto the head of her broom and then done wiggled himself inside the wicker. If he was full-growed like Slim his hidin' wouldn't a worked out well 'cause he woulda been stickin' out all over. If'n his head woulda been hidden inside the broom-head his tail and halfa his body woulda been stickin' out and if his tail woulda been curled up inside then his head woulda been stickin' out. Matter a fact, Slim was so long he coulda wrapped his body round that broom-head three or four times and still had his head and tail flappin' in the breeze whenever mama did her swingin'. Slim woulda been wrapped around that broom so tight you might've thought he belonged there like the painted snakes grandma showed me wrapped 'round those warrior spears and arrows she saved from when her tribe was free. But Shadows was little more than six inches and so he could hide his whole body inside the broomhead an' mama wouldn't of had a clue 'bout where he was.

So after awhile of just swingin' at the air mama give up and figured Shadows somehow slipped down through a crack in the floor she didn't know 'bout. She grabs me and takes me into the other room and puts me in the playpen and then she goes and starts puttin' towels under my door to make sure whatever snake creature's inside my bedroom ain't gonna get out.

Now all that woulda been fine 'cept she went and brought the broom back with her thinkin' she might need it if'n we got invaded by any more of them "slippery devils" which is what she called them.

But Shadows weren't 'bout to come out of that broom-head. In the first place he be dizzier than a weather vane spinnin in a hurricane by mama's swingin', and in the second place he was in shock from all them near hits on his wigglin' body. So he just coiled himself up inside that broom-head and tried to keep from shiverin' too much and weren't 'bout to come out 'less someone shook him out.

'Cept he couldn't stay there forever even if mama thought he be gone an' weren't 'bout to look for him. Only thing on mama's mind now was how to seal them cracks he be slippin' in and out of.

Was up to me to figure out how to get Shadows back home, and that weren't so easy bein' as now mama had me on a short leash and weren't 'bout to let me out of her sight and bein' as how Shadows weren't comin' out of that broom-head nohow 'less someone grabbed him by the neck and pulled him out.

In the meantime, mama called one of the neighbor men to come over and seal up all them cracks in the floor so no more snakes could slip in. Mr. Jones was his name, and I ain't liked him since the first time I seen him. Ain't nothin' worse than a body smellin' like sweat and stale beer and Mr. Jones had a double dose of both. He also had that hangdog look that some men seem to carry in their eyes when they get 'round women. He kept lookin' at mama like she was a rabbit and he was a starvin' coyote or somethin'. Mama didn't pay him no mind though, even made jokes at him when he tried his sweet-talkin' routine 'bout mama bein' pretty as Cleopatra and all. She told him straight out her Cleopatra looks couldn't buy her a cup of coffee 'less she had fifty cents to throw in with them sweet words and if she had a nickel for every time a man tell her she be pretty she'd be rich as Oprah by now.

I guess I coulda just sat there in my playpen listenin' to this blabbin' on and not been bothered, but Mr. Jones and his smells and bad looks got to me something awful. I forgot all 'bout Shadows and just grabbed one of my wooden alphabet blocks and tossed it at him.

I didn't aim or nothing. I just grabbed and threw.

Who'd a known I'd a hit him right between the eyes with a wooden pyramid and knocked him flat on his back?

Well, if mama didn't have 'enuff excitement for one day that done it. Mr. Jones just lay there like a lightenin' bolt hit him upside his fat head. Mama run into the kitchen to get some ice, but was me hurlin' more wooden blocks at him got him movin'. By the time mama got to him with the ice I didn't have no more blocks to throw so he was safe.

After he shook the dizziness out of his brain, he just stared at me like I was some kind of demon child and decided it was best to take his tar, oilskin paper and scraps of wood and go about the bizness of fillin' in cracks and crannies and such.

Now that I cured Mr. Jones of his hangdog disease and him and mama was busy with the cracks and the snake preventin', I returned to thinkin' 'bout Shadows who was still inside the broom-head.

Thing was, when mama be rushin' me off to the playpen, and after she got done with swingin' that broom till there weren't nothin' but air to swish at, she put the broom down right beside the playpen leanin' 'gainst the wall. It weren't far, maybe three, four feet was all, still my arms ain't never been so long as my body, and three feet was more'n I could reach.

That's the other thing you got's to know 'bout me, when I get's to concentratin on one thing, there's almost no kinda problem I can't puzzle out. So while mama an' Mr. Jones be wanderin' round the house lookin' for cracks to seal, I be sittin' in the middle of my playpen puzzlin' out how to reach across them three feet and shake Shadows out of the broom-head.

First I surveyed what I had to work with.

Weren't much in my playpen 'cept dolls and rattles and what have yous, shiny things to rattle and make noise with and hug and the like. Certainly weren't no rope to loop and throw, nor no long stick to pull that broom-head closer. Longest toy I had was a rattle on a long stick, but that weren't longer than 'bout one foot, so I was 'bout two feet short a touchin' that broom. Only thing long 'enuff to reach Shadows was the blanket I had 'round me and that weren't no good for throwin' and hookin'. Matter a fact only thing I could see with a hook on it was a wire hanger that was on the floor 'bout a foot outside my playpen.

So I sat there concentratin' on the hanger, my eyes just a'starrin' and a'starin like they weren't even mine no more.

And then it come to me.

I stuck the stick-end of the rattle through the wire mesh of the playpen and pushed and wiggled it round till I reached the hanger and pulled it toward me. Then I reached over the playpen with my rattle and stretched my arm out till it hurt and slipped the rattle inside the hanger and pulled it up. Then I tied the hanger and the rattle together with a corner of my blanket for weight and hook-ability and tossed it at the broom.

Well, I weren't no cowpoke nor bronco bustin' cowgirl so I weren't even close to catchin' that broom on my first try. And I guess if mama and Mr. Jones weren't so busy fussin' with them cracks in the floor they mighta heard what was goin' on. But I guess all they heard was my rattle rattlin' so they thought I was playin' loud is all.

I tried again, but my second throw weren't much better than the first on account of my technique.

See I was usin' a lasso-style technique I seen in one of the picture books mama got me, but this here ropin' called for a completely different kind of method than lassoin' horses and longhorn cows.

Now it just so happened one of my favorite books 'bout that time was 'bout the Chumash Indians and if'n you know one thing 'bout the Chumash they be good fishermen and they be good at harpoonin' and spearin' fish with a stick.

So it seemed to me harpoonin' might be a better technique for catchin' broom-heads than was lassoin' cows.

So that's what I done.

I tied one end of my blanket to the bar of the playpen and I took the stick of the rattle in my hand and just tried to spear the broom-head like it was a fish.

Sure weren't perfection that's for sure, and I don't know how I thought that hook was gonna catch that broom-head, but when that rattle hit that head it woke Shadows up from whatever sleep he was in. I guess he figured he was bein' whacked at again and maybe was best if he made a crawl for it while he still had the chance.

Soon as he stuck his tiny black head through the wicker and spied me smilin' he knowed was time to make his escape. He slithered out the broom-head and down the hallway and slid under the door and out into the natural world. Slim told me later, Shadows was so frightened by mama whackin' at him he kept right on slitherin' out of our neighborhood and far into the woods and took up residence with his grandparents far away from civilization.

I can't say I blame him.

Gettin' your skull almost bashed in by some madwoman bound to have a lastin' memory and motivate you to go searchin' for some new terrain for your home.

After the cracks be sealed and the snake-preventin' done, mama put another harness on me so I couldn't be wanderin' too far. I could waddle and crawl 'round alright long as it weren't outta her sight. She tied one end of the harness to the playpen and the other end to me and made sure it weren't long 'enuff to get into trouble in one of the other rooms. I could crawl alongside the walls till I got to a doorway, but that's as far as I could go. I could caterpillar and frog hop into the hallway but soon's mama seen I could reach a closet door or I could slide round a corner and slip inside a shadow and disappear she be reducin' the length of my freedom by that much more.

Try as I might, set my eyes straight as a Timicua arrow, turn the gray matter of my brain inside out and six ways to somewhere by my concentratin', there weren't nothing I could do to make the length of that harness longer or find a way to meet up with Slim again.

I don't know how long went on like this.

Two, three months I reckon, maybe longer.

Time don't run the same speed when you're one goin' on a hundred, but it was long 'enuff for me not to be crawlin' round like Slim and his clan no more, long 'enuff for me to change my entire perspective of 'The World'.

Now You Can't Imagine...

...how two feet of height'll change your perspective of 'The World'.

I mean if you been seein' everythin' 'round you from the point of view of a grasshopper and then one mornin' you woke up grown tall as a penguin; if say you were eye level to an anthill your entire life and then one day you found your self ten times taller then them ant hills and could see as high as the mountains of chairs and beds and sofas and end tables and what have yous; if say you could suddenly reach up and twist doorknobs and grab onto kitchen counters and touch stove burners and put into your mouth a hundred new flavors and shapes you never even knew existed, well you got's a whole 'nother notion of an uncharted universe you never knew was there.

When I was navigatin' 'The World' on all fours, every shiny piece of metal and button, every dust bunny and slow beetle that'd be trundlin' along the floor, every alien insect and hoary-haired spider web would hold my eye for limitless bits of time.

But when I growed some and stood up on my own two toddlin' feet and started hangin' onto tables and chairs and grabbin' onto the corners of walls and was stumblin' 'round eye level to a television, t'was a whole new continent of discoveries to be found.

If'n my mama left keys on the table, I was the first to find them and see what they could open.

I knowed there must be a keyhole in the wall where a door would let me enter a mysterious room. And I knowed if'n I tried hard 'enuff I could turn that key until it opened the door and let me into the inside.

I knowed it 'cause when I put mama's key into the door under the sink I could open it and scrunch down real little and after awhile I would become invisible. Mama could call and call and call and even when she was standin' right in front of me she couldn't see nor hear me.

Then when she leave all worried and searchin' in one of them other rooms I could use that key to open the door and become visible again and sit all happy and laughin like nothin' happened.

I could even pull myself up over kitchen tables and countertops and sinks an' hold and uncharted new landscape in my eyes. I could reach my hand over the table edge and grab onto a pork chop and an ear of corn and could get a fistful of black-eyed peas into my mouth 'fore mama even knowed I had 'em 'cept for the smeared evidence left on my face.

Yeah, mama had her harness and held the length of my explorations, but once I could

stand upright without ploppin'
down on my behind every two
seconds, that world had a height
and a dimension and a mystery
I'd never imagined when all I
could see was the soles of shoes
walking past.

'Course weren't long after my
black-eyed pea and pork chop
caper that mama figured she
better take precautions 'gainst
my new found powers and I got
welcomed rather abruptly into
the "No" world.

"No Rainbo, don't touch that!
No Rainbo, keep your hands away
from the stove! No Rainbo.
Rainbo, no! RAINBO!!! RAINBO
BWANA!!! No! No! No! No! No!"

Well, I hope to tell you, if'n
you ain't been welcomed into the

"No" world yet, you don't know what you're missin'.

I been told there's some kinda hell on the other side of heaven, but if it ain't a "No" world it ain't no kind of hell to me 'cause there ain't nothing worse than every five seconds being told "you can't", "you won't", "you never", and "don't, don't, don't, don't, don't!"

Bein' tied to my playpen on a short leash was one kind of ignominy, havin' my friend Slim banished and his nephew swatted at and almost squished like a horsefly was another, but when mama put me into the "no" world on account of my adventuresome spirit, well, that was too much.

Now I don't know nothin 'bout demons and devils and witches and the like, (Grandma Little Wolf knows about them strange seraphs of the dark), but weren't long after I got introduced to the "no" world some kind of demon started takin' possession of my body.

Call it an allergic reaction to an overdose of no's, but when my demon jumped out of my skin, she be screamin' and yellin' and throwin' a fit that no mama in the world ever want to deal with. My demon could crack mirrors and break eardrums with her screams. She could clear my playpen of every toy, could tear the eyes out of every cuddly bear, and could pull the arms off of every doll before mama could even try to hug her demonic body to her breast. My demon could swing and throw and smash more things in a Hong Kong minute than an Oklahoma tornado. And the worse thing 'bout her was she liked to show off her powers of destruction in front of a captive audience.

Put me into a grocery store with bright jars and cans and pretty boxes and tell me, "No! Don't touch that, Rainbo! No, you can't have that, Rainbo! No, I'm not gonna buy that, Rainbo!" and sure 'enuff, my demon would suddenly appear like there was a storm brewin' inside me just ready to blow through the sails of my arms and legs. She'd be kickin' and screamin' and hurlin' things down the aisles and creatin' such a wild spectacle people must of thought I was Rosemary's devil baby or an alien or somethin'.

There was another thing that happened after I got introduced to the "No" world and my demon child started showin' herself, I started figurin' out how the harness worked.

Weren't much really.

Was just a hook and a knot and a snap here and there and I was free. First time I puzzled through it I surprised myself at how easy it was.

Free!

But free to do...what?

And once free how do I not get caught for bein' free?

So first time I freed myself I took a quick survey round the perimeter of my freedom, then hooked myself back up again.

I wanted to meet up with Slim and catch up on all I missed somethin' fierce, but I'd learned mama and her broom could appear at any moment if I weren't careful and I didn't want to risk another near-snake-squishin'.

So I rehearsed my escape a few times 'fore I actually started stayin' off the leash long 'enuff to find and meet up with Slim.

The problem was how to keep mama from findin' out I was free once I was off the leash. I mean I could turn the corner and disappear out of her sight, but she knew the leash ended a few feet past the door and so I weren't really goin' nowhere. The trick was to keep her thinkin' nowhere was where I was when I was really somewhere else.

Now it just so happened I had one of them dolls that talk if'n you pull a string on their backside. And seemed to me mama didn't pay as much attention to my explorin' if'n she thought I be talkin' back and forth with that doll like we be havin' a good 'ole conversation 'bout havin' a tea party or goin' to a Cinderella ball or somethin'.

So that's what I done.

I dragged my talking doll along with me and unleashed myself and pulled the string and started carryin' on a conversation like we hadn't seen each other for years. And as I was talkin' I kept movin' farther and farther away till I was at the doorway of my mama's bedroom again lookin' across at where her clothes closet was.

Then I waited for mama's footsteps.

Nothin'!

I toddled along till I got in front of her closet and pulled the string of my talkin' doll.

Nothin'!

I opened the doors to the clothes closet and pulled the string and waited.

Nothin'!

Well, once I knowed I could do this and mama wasn't gonna come runnin' and attackin' with her broom again, I armed myself with my crack-openin' tools. When mama fed me my lunch of strained apricots and creamed spinach and put the spoon in my hand to feed myself (which I had just started to do), I pretended to let my demon child come out and tossed the spoon into my playpen.

Now I know right 'bout now you be thinking "that girl outta her mind if she thinkin' I be believin' this tall tale" (especially the part 'bout me knowin' so much when I could hardly walk and talk right), but the truth is most of what I knew I already knowed when I was born and the rest I kinda picked up by puzzlin' out and doin', so when I thought 'bout Slim and the closet and the spoon, why it all come natural how I was gonna open up a crack in the floor and meet up with Slim again.

Just so happened I got my chance on a Sunday. I remember it was a Sunday 'cause mama was gone to the Baptist Church and grandma was watchin' after me. Grandma weren't nearly so restrictin' as my mama, so I knew I'd have the time I needed to work a hole in the floor.

Wasn't much work to it really.

Just some old rug, and tar paper, and a scrap 'a wood to get through. I pried the wood up easy with my spoon handle and poked a hole through the tar paper and rug. Then I stuck my finger in the hole and wiggled it 'round.

I thought Slim would come like he done before when he saw

my finger wigglin' at him like a fat worm, but he weren't nowhere to be found. I tried puttin' my eyeball into the hole to see if maybe I could spot him, but I couldn't see nothin' 'cept the dark under the house so I laid the piece of wood over the hole and went back and locked myself in the harness.

I didn't get the opportunity to try to meet up with Slim again for another three days. Mama was sleeping from her night shift job and grandma was watching me again. I slipped out of the harness and pulled the wood aside and wiggled my finger down in the hole. Then, I pulled my finger out and waited for his head to peek up through the crack.

Well, it weren't long--but the head that peeked through the hole didn't look right. I mean the head was black and shiny like Slim's but was shaped a little different, more triangular maybe and the eyes were more red than black.

I weren't sure what was different, but I knowed something was, then when I started whisperin all excited to catch him up on all that had happened since last time I seen him, (and 'specially when I asked him 'bout what happened to Shadows), he just popped his head back down in the hole and disappeared. I stuck my finger back through the hole and wiggled, but he weren't comin'

back from where he slithered off
to.

I didn't get a chance to visit
my snake hole again till the
following Sunday when mama
was at church. This time I
brought a peace offerin' with me,
a dab of ham parfait on my
spoon which I dipped down in
the hole and wiggled 'round.

I guess the odor of home
cookin' got to him 'cause when I
lifted the spoon out of the hole
his head was stuck to it lickin'
away like it was a strawberry
jubilee. I knew right then weren't
Slim though 'cause he was 'bout
half Slim's size and just stared
at me blank and confused when
I went into my whisperin'
routine. Then he starts to turn
his head this way and that like

he's got an antenna on top of his head and is tryin' to tune into my frequency. Finally his head stops movin' and he just stares straight back like he hit the right channel.

"You're the one my brother told me about, aren't you?" he whispers in a deep suspiratin' voice.

"Your brother, Slim?"

"Half. We have different fathers."

"How is he? I haven't seen him since--"

"Not doing so well...rat poison."

"He ate rat poison?"

"Didn't eat it. Ate a rat ate rat poison. Happens. You humans always trying to exterminate one creature or another. Don't think much about all the others you're exterminating with them."

"Is he...is he gonna be all right?"

"Don't know. Seems to be getting better, but it's hard to tell. He just sleeps mostly."

"Is there anything--"

"No."

"Oh, I'm--"

"I know who you are."

"--Rainbo. What's--?"

"Who I am isn't important."

"But I'd like to be... ah... friends."

"I have friends."

"I know, but...human friends."

"I don't need human friends."

"Oh...well...ah, tell Slim I'm sorry, okay...for my mother...She liked to scare him an' your nephew half to death."

"Wasn't your fault according to my brother."

"Yeah. No. Mama's crazy with snakes. Thinks they're all serpents conspirin' with the devil. Says if you touch one you're gonna go to hell."

"Human fallacy. Elders say humans were created from the mud and that's why they hate earthly creatures. Think they're better than the mud and any creature that lives close to the earth. Always trying to reach for the stars and become creatures of the sky like birds and angels to escape their mud-born birth. My brother believes we can change the way humans see us by showing them how we really are, not like all them lies that's been passed on about us. I don't."

"Them lies is what keeps people goin'. There's a preacher gets my mama all fired up every Sunday with snake-badness. She says all snakes in the good book is evil. Says 'only good snake is a dead snake'."

"Your mother and that book of hers is why we hide in shadows every time we feel a human's steps coming across the ground."

"You ain't much for humans are you?"

"Ain't much to be *for*."

"We ain't all bad you know, no more than snakes all bad."

"Snakes don't hurt other creatures, 'less to survive. We live according to the natural order. Humans live in an ill-conceived world of their own creation outside the natural order."

"Grandma Little Wolf says the Great Spirit cast humans out of the circle of life when the white man crossed the ocean."

"White-skins are mud-born same as any other skin. Only reason they hate the earth more is because they see themselves as above the dark ground from which they came."

"She says if it weren't for the ghost dance the native peoples would still inhabit most of the earth."

"Perhaps. Elders say the native peoples once lived in communion with our kind. But that was a long time ago. Now we die of rat poison and pesticides and lies...

I'll tell my brother you were sorry."

And with that he was gone, dartin' back through my snake hole and into the shadows.

I leaned down real close to the hole to see where he went, when suddenly he almost pokes my eye out with his head poppin' back up.

"By the way, they call me Shadey, King Shadey 'cause my father was a king," then he dove back down through the hole and was gone.

I didn't expect to see King Shadey or Slim again. Shadey didn't like humans and Slim was sick, maybe even dying.

I felt sad, like there had been some kinda empty space created inside me where the snake tribe used to live. I wanted to call Shadey back and have Slim be well and have their brothers and sisters and cousins and Elders come back and fill that hole with their presence again.

But I knew that time was past.

If'n we was ever gonna be friends again it was gonna haveta be in a different time and place and under completely different circumstances than meetin' through cracks in the floor and snake-whisperin and rememberin' misconceived stories from the book of King James.

So I Forgot...

...about Slim and Shadey and the snake family for awhile.

I had a new discovery goin' on in my head that got my blood circulatin' sideways: Writin': Namin': Makin' pictures from letters and sounds.

Now you might think holdin' a handful of alphabet letters 'bout as interestin' as holdin' the face of some sandy stone, but when I put them letters in my lap and they invented a sound and a thing I never knew before, well that was just as good as visitin' with the snake family or throwin' them alphabet blocks at Mr. Jones.

I mean I weren't no genius for words mind you.

I learned them just as hard as you learned them probably, 'cept maybe I had a talent for creatin' new ones where there weren't none and maybe was a prodigy for 'breviatin' and distillin' words down to their essential letters like LOL and IOU and URI and such.

'Course this didn't happen all in one night nor even in the seven days mama say it took God to create the stars and the planets and all the assorted creatures that congregate on them. No, this happened after mama teach me day after day each letter had its own special sound and showed me how "A" was for "apple" and "B" was for

113

"bee" and so on till we got to "Z" for "zebra".

And I probably wouldn't have learned nothin' if'n it weren't for them pictures and mama repeatin' how them letters belonged to them particular beings over and over.

But the thing was, once I learned the secret of namin', well, I knew I held the gift of creation in my hands.

I mean I could lay them alphabet blocks on the floor and turn them this way and that and come up with all kinds of curious combinations of creatures.

You remember that adventure I told you 'bout when I found mama's keys and opened all them secret doors, well, that weren't nothin' compared to when I discovered her lipstick on the table and started begettin' a whole new world on the walls.

I mean I drew a whole herd of pink elephants and named them "Elepinks" and weren't no one could say it weren't so.

I drew dog-cows and monkey-horses and banana-lilies and gave them names like "cowpoodle" and "monksie" and "bananalily".

I wrote "mama mama mama mama mama" five times over till it was like there was a tall row of mamas standin' there smilin'.

I wrote my name and the names of all my great Timicua grandparents like "Fire-In-The-Light" and "Coyote-Standing-On-

The-Mountain" and "Eyes-Like-A-Spotted-Owl" and the names of every friend, relative and neighbor I ever remembered and every name mama ever told me was a name.

I wrote "pee-pee" and "ca-ca" and "ding-dong" and "dumdee-deedum" upside down and backwards across the whiteness and no one knowed better 'cause they be thinkin' I was playin' all nice and quiet and was too girly-girly to conjure up such mischief in my head.

I let my eyes go wild and drew my daddy's face on a jack o'lantern and on a pig's head and on a goat with a hippopotamus' behind. (I gave them names too, but I ain't gonna tell you what they were 'cause yous might get in trouble if'n you ever say them out loud, besides that part was personal and don't have no place in this here story.)

Call me crazy if'n you want, but it didn't matter none to me if my names went with the pictures or if my picture was so new and original no one had a name for it, 'cause names ain't nothing but somebody else's idea of the way 'The World' should be and I had my own vision percolatin' in my head of how 'The World' was.

"Course I weren't much for spellin' in those days so them names was original even without my conjurin'. If'n I heard a word a certain way why that's how I spelled it.

Now you probably don't know this, but here's the thing 'bout spellin'.

Say mama be talkin' 'bout ice cream. Maybe she ask me if'n I want ice cream or if'n I don't and what flavor I want—chocolate, or strawberry, or vanilla.

So you thinks I'm gonna repeat the whole kitankaboodle back to her?

No sirree. I'm just gonna say the essence of the thing--choco or berry or nilla--so when I go's to spell it I'm gonna do the same. And then I'm gonna draw a picture of a strawberry cone with a big 'ole gob of red berry ice cream spillin' out the sides and name it BAA-BER-REE 'cause that's the way it sounds.

So that's what I done that day I found my mama's ruby red lipstick.

I wrote and drew and conjured and by time the sun disappeared from my window, I had a whole zoo livin' on the walls like that Dr. Zeuss book I was readin' 'bout the cat in the hat.

Weren't nothing to it really, 'cause of my powers of concentratin' and all. Mama say she turn her back on me for five minutes and Lord knows what mischief I could get myself into, but weren't no five minutes 'cause I knowed it takes longer for the sun to move from my chair to my bed and out my window, besides mama was conversin' in the livin' room with her friend Bertha and when them two gets their jaws a'flappin they don't stop for an hour or two, and this day them jaws was a'jabberin somethin' fierce.

'Course I knew mama was comin' at me 'fore she took two steps, even if she was tryin' to be sneaky.

I knew it 'cause I knew how much the quiet got her suspicious.

See mama learned if'n it be too quiet in my room for awhile, well, I must be in some kind of trouble or be mischief-makin'. But when she open my door and see all them ruby red creatures gazin' back at her from the walls she nearly jumped out of her shoes from the shock.

"Oh my God!!! Oh, my God. Rainbo! Rainbo, what you done, child, what have you done!!!"

Now I woulda thought mama mighta said somethin' 'bout my artistic talents and how I was a child prodigy like that Vincent guy who got so famous he cut off his ear so people would know he was really serious 'bout his art and maybe even a genius, but mama was more interested in what was left of her stick of lipstick and all the work she had to do to wipe them red creatures and names off the wall.

When grandma seen my drawings though, she said I had the gift of conjurin'.

"You've been given a gift, Rainbo, the power to bring spirit visions to life."

"But mama call me "a little devil" for what I done."

"Your mama can't see the spirit world 'cause she lives so much in the material world. When the eyes live in that world too long, they forget how to see beyond the surface of things."

"Mama say there ain't nothin' deeper than what the hands can make out o' two wooden nickels and some hard work."

"Your mama doesn't see how those two nickels have faces the same as anything else her hands can make. Did I ever tell you the story of your great grandmother, Bear-Running-Up-

The-Mountain, and how she saved our tribe?"

"You said you wished you had the gift of conjurin' like your mother once."

"But I didn't tell you her story?"

"No."

"Well, one winter, a long, long time ago, before the Great Trail burned with blood and tears and our tribe still lived in the plains where the wild buffalo wandered, the white people came to build towns on the plains and the cavalry pushed us up into the mountains. But even that wasn't enough to fill their hunger. The blue coats started coming after us and hunting us down like deer and so we had to hide in caves. If we came out of the sacred caves the blue coats would find and take us prisoners or shoot us.

"There wasn't any food way up in the mountains where the caves were. A few black bears, mountain lions, and elk, but not enough to feed the whole tribe through the long winter. Night after night the hunters come back with nothing but hard luck to show from their day of hunting. We prayed to the Great Spirit, burned sagebrush and chanted for good spirits to give us the gift of a bear or an elk, but when the snows came again and the last of our food was gone the oldest and the youngest among us began to pass on to the other world.

"Then one evening, Bear-Running-Up-The-Mountain, who was just a girl, barely a little older than you, woke up in the middle of the night with a great vision. The cave was dark as a closed eye and everyone was asleep but Bear-Running-Up-The-Mountain saw the light of many creatures in her vision and picked up a stick of charred manzanita branch from the fire and began to draw the creatures in her vision on the cave walls.

"She drew elk and deer and mountain goats. She drew herds of great buffalo and flocks of wild turkeys. She drew fires in the caves and great gatherings of chiefs and peoples from different tribes. She drew Lakota and Piute and Apache gathered

125

round the fire and feasting on the sacred animals of the earth. And when she had finished drawing the last figure she fell into a deep, deep sleep.

"As the sun broke over the cave mouth and the tribe began to wake one by one Bear-Running-Up-The-Mountain's vision glowed from the walls. Each animal she drew came alive in the light, running through the flickering shadows of the morning fire and the morning sun. The tribe knew Bear-Running-Up-The-Mountain's vision was a great good omen and as the hunters slung their bows over their shoulders and slid their arrows into their harnesses they were renewed with optimism as they trudged through the heavy snow to find food for the tribe.

"That evening when the hunters returned they brought many elk and deer with them from the hunt and the tribe had a great feast in honor of Bear-Running-Up-The-Mountain.

"Our tribe survived that winter and the next three winters and as Bear-Running-Up-The-Mountain's reputation grew so did her visions. Chiefs and shamans from other tribes began to journey to our cave to visit the young girl with the "eyes of the Great Spirit in her dreams". Soon the entire cave walls of our tribe were filled with her visions and then she began to draw her visions in the surrounding caves as well. For the first time since the great beginning, different tribes and peoples began to live side by side in the caves hidden from the bluecoats and the white man's civilization. On her twelfth birthday she was to pass through to the other side and the Elders would offer her the blue flame of the Great Spirit and she would become the high priestess of our tribe.

"But then Chief Crazy Horse had "The Ghost Dance" vision and all the tribes began ignoring Bear-Running-Up-The-Mountain's visions. Since the Ghost Dance foretold the white man's fall and the Native Peoples returning to their lands the hunters no longer went out to hunt game to store food for the coming winter. The chiefs and shaman and hunters sat and smoked peace pipes and made sacrifices of buffalo in honor of the Great Spirit and waited for the Ghost Dance to come.

Bear-Running-Up-The-Mountain's visions were forgotten because she did not dream a Ghost Dance vision, but instead dreamed the whites growing and growing all around us like bad seeds. She became delirious and did not bathe and wandered around speaking to the voices in her head. She moved into a small cave by herself away from the native peoples and drew her visions of impending doom.

On the night of her twelfth birthday, she screamed out so loud in her dreaming that all the native peoples woke and ran to her cave. There they saw Bear-Running-Up-The-Mountain lost in the sleep-of-death. Shaman danced and burned herbs and secret potions to wake her from her death-in-life, but nothing roused her. Some said she had passed on to the other world because a demon spirit had possessed her and given her evil dreams. On the walls of her cave was the most horrific vision the native peoples had ever seen, drawn on the night before she had fallen into the sleep-of-death:

Winter. Great mounds of snow everywhere. Bodies of native peoples and animals strewn on the ground, frozen, half-buried in whiteness. A blizzard swirling. Black clouds. Fires ashen smudges on the walls, long dead, and gathered round the extinguished fires, the frozen peoples brushed with frost, their faces hoary, ice. And eyes everywhere, looking down like stars, but not flickering, not eyes lit with fire, eyes still, open, dreaming the dream of seasons that do not change nor new suns drive away, eyes still as stones sleeping in shadow and unable to remember.

At first when the native peoples saw this vision they were terrified and began to wonder if the Ghost Dance vision were true, but Bright-Eagle, one of the shaman, said that an evil spirit had taken possession of Bear-Running-Up-The-Mountain's body and given her this terrible vision.

He said he would prepare a strong potion to cast out the evil spirit and spread it over her body.

For three days Bear-Running-Up-The-Mountain remained in her sleep-of-death, then on the fourth day she awoke. She did not remember her visions and was surprised at the drawings on her cave walls. She never remembered painting her visions or even having the visions. She awoke without visions or memories, her special gift gone. She did not speak, nor could she see and when her mother tried to speak to her she did not hear her but rose and walked out of her cave and continued walking up the mountain path till she was gone.

No one went to help her for fear that they too would be possessed by an evil spirit who would take away their eyes and tongue and make them sleep the sleep-of- death. She wandered away and no one saw her again. But the next morning, when the tribe went outside, there was a huge painting on the cliff face. The picture showed the whole tribe ghost dancing in the other world, a vision foretelling what was to come."

With that, grandma took out a stick of sagebrush and lit it on fire and waved the smoke 'round to rid the room of any bad spirits that might have been awakened from her story.

"Grandma, you didn't finish the story."

"The story's done little one. There's nothing else to tell."

"But what happened?"

"Bear-Running Up-The-Mountain's vision came true. That winter almost all of the tribe froze or starved to death waiting for the Ghost Dance to happen. But the white man did not leave the native lands, nor did a great death rise among them. Instead they grew and grew like locusts and pushed the tribes farther and farther into the mountains or took them as prisoners where they died of diseases and a sickness of the heart. The few that survived left the caves and found Bear-Running sitting atop an enormous boulder that had the face of an eagle. She was blind now, only the world of her

134

visions alive in her sight. When the last of the Elders asked her to help the survivors of her tribe, she got up and walked down the mountain. She led them into the gates of Fort Sumner where the blue coats took them into custody."

"That ain't no good story, grandma," I tells her. "If that's the gift you says I got's I don't want it. Seems like nothing but bad luck and heartache comes of it to me."

"Maybe you just didn't understand the story, Rainbo. Many tribes disappeared because of the Ghost Dance vision. And many were taken by the cold and the scarcity of food when they hid up in the mountains away from the blue coats. Your great grandmother's gift saved our tribe through three terrible winters and saved the remainder of our tribe from being hunted down by the soldiers. If it weren't for her, I wouldn't be telling you her story now. None of us would even be here. Not me, nor your mama, nor you, nor the thousands of other native peoples who owe their lives to her gift of seeing. She went into the other world to show us how to live in this world. And maybe that's the reason you got the gift too, Rainbo, to take us all to another place, a better place that we haven't even seen yet."

Well, that last little bit got to me.

So what if grandma was half-crazy with that spirit vision stuff and sometimes it was awful hard to tell what was real or what she just wanted to imagine, 'cause I liked to draw creatures on the walls with mama's lipstick and if someone thought I was evokin' animal spirits and foretellin' the future, well more power to them. It didn't matter much to me one way of the other. Besides, I'm goin' back 'bout ten years here so things mighta happened a little different then the way I'm sayin', and who knows how grandma woulda told the story if'n it were her doin' the tellin'.

I still like to draw on walls with my mama's ruby red lipstick, and give my own names to 'The World', and it don't have nothing to do with whether they have magical powers or not.

And I still have strange dreams that no one but grandma can explain with any kind of meanin'.

And if I didn't have some kind of special gift, well I wouldn't be famous and I wouldn't be writin' this story in the first place, which brings me to what I wanted to say to begin with.

Grandma Was A Curandera

She was a curandera before she became a snake-woman, and if it wasn't for the forgetfulness disease she'd still be a curandera.

Now I know some people think curanderas are akin to devils, sorcerers and the like, but grandma couldn't have exorcised you from a possession if she knew the demon's name and held him up by the scruff of his neck.

She might throw some wart powder on him, or give him a bad case of the Itching Sickness. But pulling spirits out of a person's insides like she had a magnet in her mouth was beyond her realm.

No, grandma mostly conjured cures for the human heart. She was known as the Curandera-of-Alachua and people drove down from Southern Georgia and up from the Florida Keys to have her create a potion or a remedy for their ills.

She made ointments for the blues, liniments for birthdays and funerals, salves to heal the love-struck and the star-crossed, elixirs for the cursed. She concocted good luck potions that would have you trip over silver dollars raining from a storm-blackened sky, and lotions that could erase pock-mocks deep as moon craters from your face. She mixed ground rattlesnake rattles and sassafras buds for infertile wombs, and created babies out of aphrodisiac dust of rosemary and thyme. She gathered herbs and bones, fragrances and nuances, and read the speckles in your eyes to find your own special cure.

She would've been mixing potions and curing people till she was ninety like her mother and grandmother before her, but one morning she woke up with the forgetfulness seed blossoming in her brain.

Now forgetfulness is a strange creation, personal as a thumbprint. Grandma's was like a Venus Flytrap with a special craving for plants. Once the seed took root, Forgetfulness'es many mouths snapped up the shapes of leaves and the fragrances of flowers in her mind. She couldn't remember which herb went with which potion--how many lavender buds went with how so many pinches of Saint Wort's dust to make a cure for unrequited love. When she did remember whole potions, sometimes she forgot what they were for.

"Is tumeric for indigestion or the blues?" she wondered one morning holding the white flower in her palm.

"Is this lemongrass or goosegrass?" turning leaf-blades in an afternoon sun.

"A squirrel's bone-dust or the ground up scales of a rattlesnake's skin?"

Subtleties were lost. The grey and tan shades of each creatures' bones; the similar but different leaf patterns between poison oak and prickly lettuce.

Yet some mornings she woke up clear and lucid, as if the flower of forgetness wilted in her sleep. She could remember each nuanced difference as if she were holding that flower or leaf or pinch of dust for the first time.

On those mornings, she'd write down her potions in an old curandera book. She drew sketches of each plant, bone, and seed she mixed together for basic healing--sassafras and thyme; lizard toes and persimmon dust; rattlesnake fang and porcupine bone.

But as the flower grew larger in her brain, the names in the book became as disconnected as strands of seaweed floating on the surface of the sea. Her potions turned into a mismatched jumble of names, pictures, textures and smells she couldn't attach to what she held in her hands; recipes with instructions her mind couldn't follow, or that sat before her like hieroglyphic pages she could no longer read.

People forgave her forgetfulness—at first, anyway.

She was a conjurer after all, a wise-woman from an extinct tribe, a Timicua curandera in an age of doctors and scientists. Her exotic oddness was the mystery of her magic.

Besides, even among curanderas, grandma was known as an improviser. She'd add a dash of this or that herb or dust to zing a standard love potion, throw in a pinch of yarrow to heal a fractured heart. When people came to grandma, they didn't expect the exact cure for what they asked. What they wanted was something more, something special, something uniquely personal which only grandma could give them.

What they didn't expect though, was a potion to attract Mister or Miss Right to suddenly afflict them with a hunger for dark chocolate, or a liniment to keep their newborn healthy to cause a torrent of grief as they gazed into their baby's eyes.

After a few mistaken potions though, the word spread, and people stopped coming to grandma for potions. She'd sit on her porch and wait, fussing with her recipes and pouches of ingredients, but fewer and fewer people came, and then none at all.

She'd sit, drowse in a dream, watch buffalo graze in the reflection of her mind.

Then, one afternoon while she was waiting, a man in a suit came with a piece of paper that said she couldn't live in her house any more because the bank wanted the money she forgot to pay. Since she had no money and people didn't need her potions anymore, she packed up her possessions and got on a bus to Oakville.

Home, Where
The Buffaloes
No Longer Roam

"That Greyhound was about as comfortable as riding on a porcupine's back. And I didn't see a single buffalo. Not one."

I grabbed her bags and helped her down the bus's stairs.

"Buffaloes don't live in Tennessee, grandma. They live in North Dakota."

"North Dakota. That's a long way away."

"Are you hungry?"

"No. When did they leave?"

"I don't know. Before I was born, I guess. I always thought they lived there."

"In Dakota? No. They were roamers, roamed wherever there was grass to graze. You've grown so tall since the last time."

"Mama says I'm a bean sprout."

"You're sprouting alright. Thirteen?"

"Eleven."

"Eleven. What potions have I taught you?

"Ah...none, grandma. You said I was too young."

"I've never shown you how to make a potion?"

"You showed me how to get rid of a wart once. Here. On my thumb."

"I should've put more invisible salve on it, get rid of the mark. I told you where warts come from didn't I?"

"Toads."

"No. Before the toads?"

"I didn't know there was a before?"

"There's always a before, Rainbo. Even before the before there's a before."

"You mean in the beginning, when the First Peoples lived."

"Yes, when all the Earth was a seed. If you took the wart off your thumb and planted it in the ground, that wart turned into an animal, and that's how all the different animals of the world were created."

"Like Darwin."

"Darwin?"

"Evolution. I'm learning about him in school. Survival of the species. How dinosaurs are really birds and stuff."

"Birds were never dinosaurs. Those schools, they've always been teaching that. Facts. Their history. But the essence, Rainbo,

that's not in their school books.
What makes a toad a toad and
not a fish or a bird. That never
changes, and that they can't
teach. You sure I've never told
you about potion-making?"

"Yes, grandma."

"Then we need to start. What
do you know about plants?"

"I know what Poison Oak
looks like."

"Good. The shape and color of
leaves. That's an essence."

"You want me to be *like* you're
curandera-in-training, grandma,
like The Sorcerer's Apprentice?"

"Apprentice, yes, like that, my
little curandera."

We walked silently to our
house after that. When we got
there, I put grandma's bags down
in my bedroom, and poured her

a glass of iced tea. We went outside and sat on the porch because it was cooler there. Every now and then a breeze played on the eucalypti leaves like someone was plucking a guitar string made out of straw. Then grandma got up and started walking toward the sound.

"Grandma? Grandma, where are you going?"

She didn't answer till I caught up to her.

"Grandma?"

She wasn't there, not there standing beside me in our front yard. She was somewhere else, somewhere she couldn't quite remember, somewhere her mind took her.

"I heard hooves, Rainbo, walking slowly across the grass, meandering, grazing. They're just on the other side of those eucalypti."

"What?"

"Buffalo."

"No, grandma, there's a highway there.

"I can hear them. Listen."

"That's the sound of trucks and cars. Come on, I'll show you."

I locked my hand in hers and we walked to the other side of the stand. We stepped through an arch of brush and stood in front of a chain-linked fence. Cars whooshed past on the highway.

"See?"

She looked, but she didn't see. It was like we'd taken a detour into another world, one she couldn't imagine was suddenly there.

It wasn't real. Not for her. Not for what she was hearing in her mind. In that world, there were buffalo grazing. She had heard the direction of the sound wrong, that's all. The buffalo were somewhere else, somewhere off in another direction.

"Let's go back, Rainbo. They're not here."

When mama came home from work later that night, they talked at the kitchen table while I finished my homework, and then grandma lay her blanket on the floor over a mat she'd brought with her.

She didn't sleep in the bed we made up. She just gazed up at the plaster ceiling glittering with speckled stars and hummed a song. She said she'd rather be outside in our back yard singing to real stars, but being on account of her arthritis and the moistness in the night air, it was better she slept inside.

Mama wouldn't have let her sleep outside, even if she wanted, because of her wandering. She didn't want grandma getting lost.

"She doesn't remember Oakville the way she used to, besides the town's changed with all the new buildings. Watch her close, Rainbo. Your grandma is in a changing time."

I Didn't Know Nothing
Till I Heard The Stars...

"If you listen real close, Rainbo, you can hear the stars whisper your name."

Now I never heard of no stars having a conversation like me and my snake-friend Slim, and I thought it must be because of her bad memory that she had a mind for such notions.

But she kept on about it and when I tried to change the subject by talking about something she might remember, (like this morning's breakfast of apple fritters and hominy grits), she shushed me and told me to close my eyes and listen real close.

"What do star whispers sound like, grandma?

"The way wind sounds before it becomes a wind."

Grandma often spoke in such wisdom-riddles. Sometimes you couldn't see her meaning till it slept inside your brain for awhile and woke up as a familiar face in a dream. Sometimes her meaning jumped into the middle of another thought a day or a week later. And sometimes she would tell a second wisdom riddle which explained the first.

"Like a cloud, Rainbo, like a cloud whispering to the sky. Now, just close your eyes and listen, child."

But as hard as I tried, all I heard were cars whooshing by on the highway and dogs barking at night shadows running past their yards. There wasn't even a guitar-playing cricket to give the stars a melody to whisper by.

Strange how if you scrunch your eyes real tight, you can suddenly see the stars inside your head. Were these the stars I was supposed to hear, or were they the ones above us as we sat outside on the porch? Or maybe the ones inside my head were whispering to the ones outside and that's the conversation I was supposed to hear?

I listened and I listened and after a long while, the cars faded and the dogs went to sleep and there was nothing left but our breathing and the wind playing through the oaks.

And then after a time our breathing and the wind died

down and a silence came, a silence so loud I wondered how I'd never heard such a thunderous silence before.

And through the silence I heard another sound, more than a sound but a voice really, voices, one and then another and then so many I couldn't hear anything except that chorus of sounds, as many voices as there were stars, all whispering together like they were a great orchestra with each star playing their own instrument.

"Rainbo...Rainbo...Rainbo..."

I can't tell you how long I listened out there on our porch looking up at those millions and millions of stars. It must've been for hours though, because grandma was gone by the time I woke from my listening, and the sky was changing to a blue the color of a robin's egg, and those twinkling candles celebrating the birth of day dimmed out one by one.

I sat outside with grandma and listened to the stars most every night after that and sometimes when she wasn't feeling so good I came outside to listen alone.

Other Books
In The _You Don't Know Me_
Series

Book Two
When You Put Your Head
In A Crocodile's Mouth

Book Three
Live To Fly

Book Four
When Your Power Animal
Speaks To You

Book Five
When You Are On
A Vision Quest

www.ingramcontent.com/pod-product-compliance
Lightning Source LLC
Chambersburg PA
CBHW022127170626
46808CB00002B/872